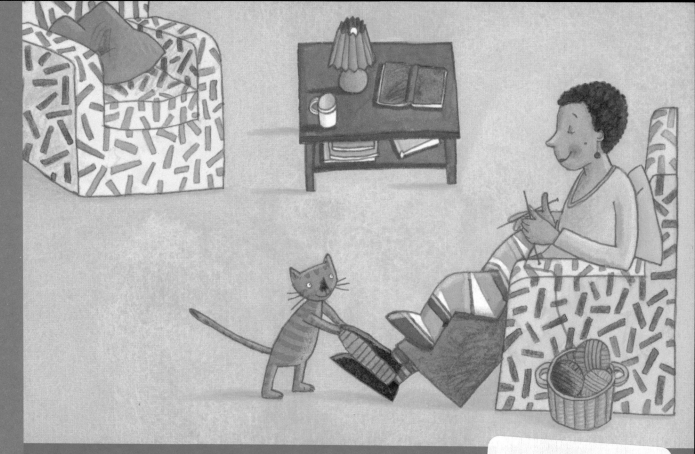

Mommy knits a scarf.

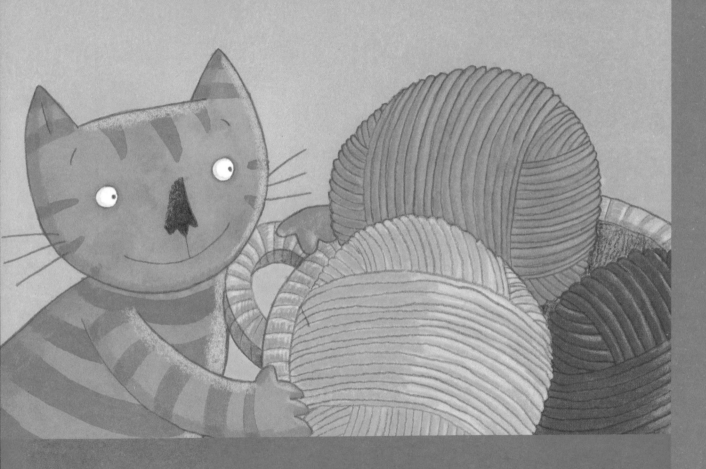

Tabby Cat finds the yarn.

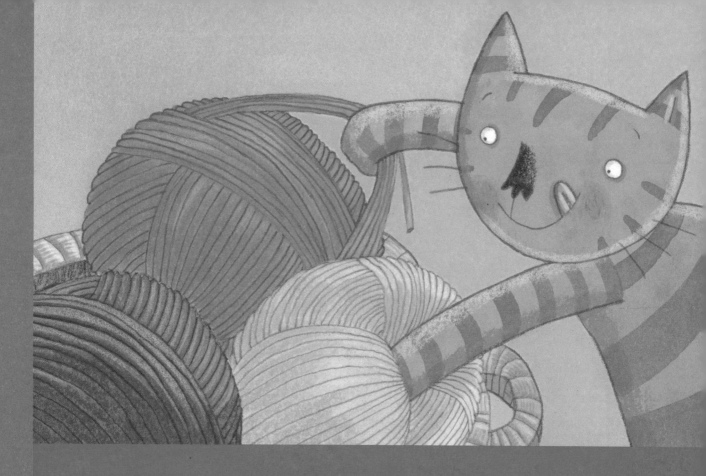

Tabby Cat grabs the yarn.

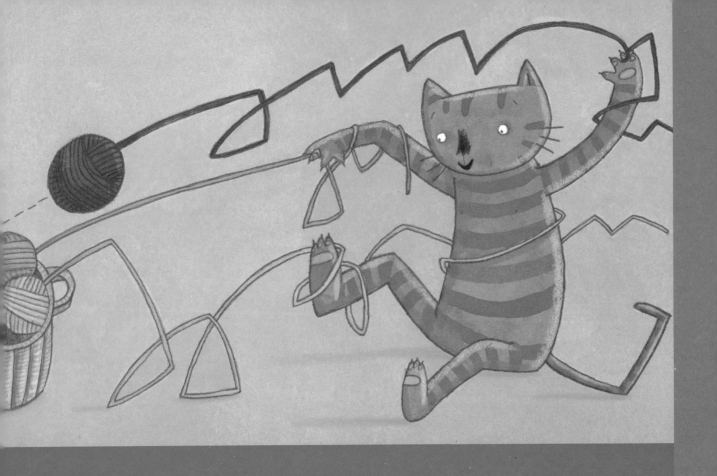

Tabby Cat pulls the yarn.

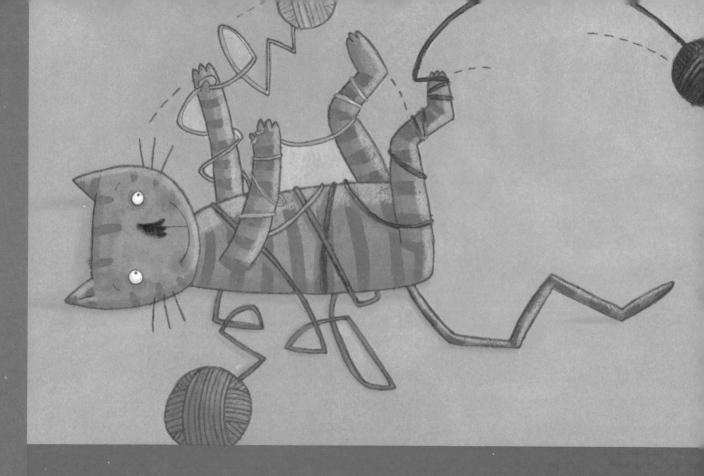

Tabby Cat throws the yarn.

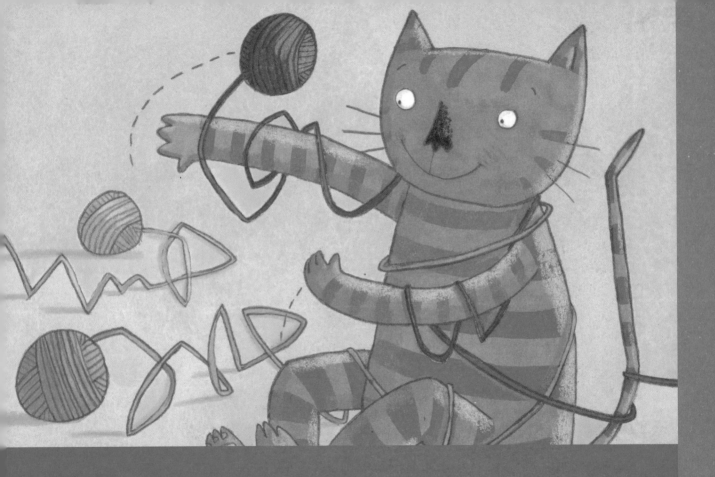

Tabby Cat loops the yarn.

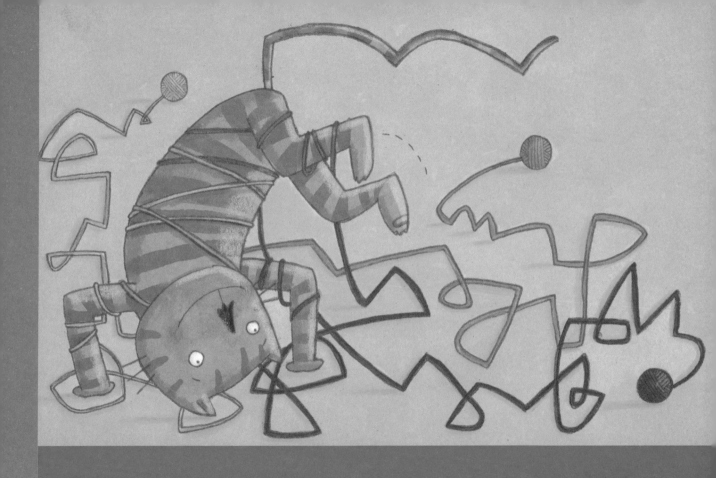

Tabby Cat rolls in the yarn.

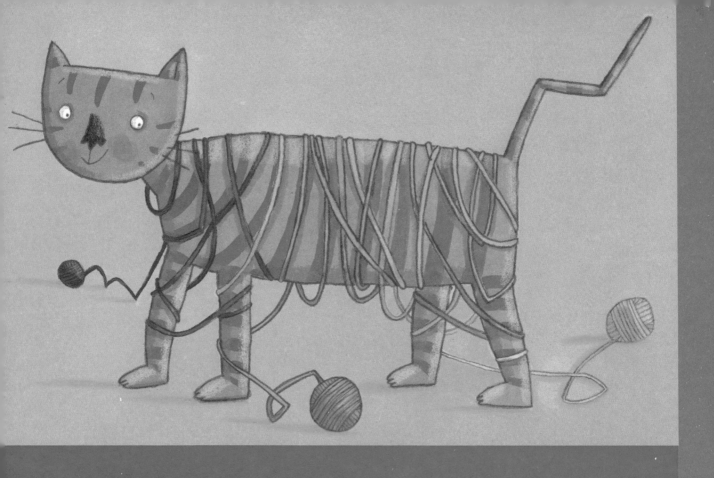

Now Tabby Cat has a scarf.